About Hey, Don't Forget the Sunscreen!

"What a terrific message to send to kids! I wish I knew about skin cancer as a child and to wear sun block. I myself had a basal cell on my nose at age 45. This is such an important message to children!"

—Dr. Jeffrey Stein, Internal Medicine,
Board Certified, Boca Raton, Florida

"I am very passionate about preventative health care, especially with respects to sunscreening. I discuss this subject every day with all of my patients and their parents. After having a patient diagnosed with melanoma, I continue to preach the benefits of sunscreening and reapplying sunscreen everyday to prevent skin cancer! I would recommend this book to all of my patients and their parents!"

—Norina B. Ocampo, MD, FAAP, board certified
pediatrician, graduate from Georgetown University
School of Medicine, former resident at the MUSC Children's Hospital

Cover and interior design by James Mensidor
Illustrations by JZ Sagario

Published in the United States of America

ISBN: 978-1546608080
1. Juvenile Fiction / Health & Daily Living / General
2. Juvenile Fiction / Education see School & Education
17.07.08

Dedication

I would like to dedicate this book to my
sisters, Pam and Rosie, who always inspired
me to draw, write, laugh, and sing to
my heart's content! Keep your
inner child alive and happy in
spite of your age! Love
and miss you.

Hi! Let me introduce myself. My name is Stacey. Today is Sunday and we are shopping at the local grocery store like we usually do. I look forward to seeing my friends. They shop there too! There's John with his aunt Donna by the ice cream case. When I get closer, I see John's aunt has a bandage on her face. I look up and politely ask what is wrong.

She simply said, "When I was your age,
I played unprotected in the sun for too long."
I said, "We read in school that the sun helps
our bodies make vitamin D, which helps fight
disease and helps keep our bones strong!"

"That's true," she said, "but you still need protection from the ultraviolet rays, even on those cool and cloudy days."
So I asked Aunt Donna, "What's the bandage for?"
She pointed to her nose and said she had a sore, one that wouldn't go away, so she made an appointment with her doctor one day.

So what's the big deal? Aunt Donna called it skin cancer, and it's damage from the sun. There are three forms, and it can affect anyone: basal cell, squamous cell carcinoma, and melanoma.

"I would like to learn more! What is the difference, and what can I do to protect myself from sun damage?" She said, "I have basil cell. It grows on the surface of the skin. This type of sun damage is most common."

"And there is **squamous** cell carcinoma. If not treated, it can go beyond the surface to other parts of the body. Melanoma is the most **dangerous** if not treated. It is also hereditary, which means it can be found in the family genes. "

Aunt Donna continued, "So this is what you can do to be proactive. First, you should never smoke! That you already know. It makes your skin age fast and heal very slowly. Then, always apply water resistant SPF (sun protection factor) 30 before you go out in the sun, and reapply every two hours. But there's more to be done!

You'll also need a hat for your head. Don't forget your eyes need attention—some cool shades with UVA and UVB protection."

"So how do I get my vitamin D?" I asked.
Aunt Donna replied, "Small amounts of sun exposure,
along with your sunscreen, helps manufacture all
the vitamin D your body needs! Enriched orange
juice, milk, and salmon also help. And a
one-a-day multi-vitamin would be good for you!

So as we said goodbye with a kiss and a hug, I promised Aunt Donna I would pass this lesson on. Don't be afraid to go out and have fun, but just make sure you have protection from the sun!

Made in the USA
Coppell, TX
21 April 2021

54275249R00019